Providence

God's Care for the Lost Sheep

By: Magda Woods

Providence: God's Care for the Lost Sheep
Written by Magda Woods

Foreword by Jeremy G. Woods

FaithVenture Media - *www.faithventuremedia.com*
Târgu Mureş, România

"But without faith it is impossible to please Him, for he who comes to God must believe that He is, and that He is a rewarder of those who diligently seek Him." Hebrews 11:6 NKJV

Descrierea CIP a Bibliotecii Naţionale a României
WOODS, MAGDA
Providence : God's care for the lost sheep / Magda Woods. - Târgu-Mureş : Faithventure Media, 2017
ISBN 978-606-94447-1-9

2

Endorsement

Magda Woods has taken a simple, delightful story of a young boy searching for his forever family to remind the reader about God's plan and purpose for each of us. We know God has absolute control, but He has a divine plan for each of us to work out through His leading. Most importantly, this story is for all ages. Young people and adults will be able to relate to the young orphan boy James searching for something that was so strong in his heart. We all are seekers, and this story is just another way of showing us that God is leading us to that perfect peace in Him.

Barbara Glenn
MSC Mission Mobilizer
North American Mission Board

Dedication

First of all, I would like to dedicate this book to God, the One who deserves all the glory. He is so full of love towards us that He gave His only Son so that we can find salvation through Jesus. I want His name to be honored throughout the pages of this book. As the title says, God is taking care of each of us, as we have all been lost sheep at a certain point in our lives, but He found us and changed us through His overwhelming grace that is sufficient for us. May we all live our lives according to His Will and bring Him honor as His children, who have been adopted through Jesus in His eternal family!

I also would like to dedicate this book to my wonderful husband, who I love and respect. He is a great blessing from God for my life, and I am very thankful for how God wonderfully directed our paths so that we met and started the journey of life together. He is a great encouragement for me on the writing side as well, and as this is my first book to officially publish. I am very glad of all the support I have received from him, as he is already a very experienced author.

This book is also dedicated to our baby that has as a due date January 1st, 2018. Both my husband and I are very pleased with God's gift of life that grows in my womb, and we are just very blessed to be parents even from now. It is God's miracle of life, and may God help us to be responsible parents that will bring our child closer to Him through our own example and teachings, as we desire that our first child, and all children that God will give us, will follow Him with all their hearts and with perseverance.

This book is also dedicated to all readers, of all ages, and may each of you find encouragement as you go through the pages of this book. May you trust God more and more in your everyday lives, as He is mighty and can do much more than we think or imagine. He is able to do anything that He wants because He has all the power in Heaven and Earth. To Him be the glory and praise!

Table of Contents

Foreword

By Jeremy G. Woods

God's providence is clearly shown in how He works in the lives of the unsaved even before they come to know Christ, and God provides for His children as a shepherd cares for his sheep. When a sheep goes astray, the shepherd leaves the others to look for the lost sheep, and this is the same with the Great Shepherd, Jesus.

The novel, Providence, is similar to a parable that Jesus told, the parable of the Lost Sheep. In the book, James, an orphan boy, plans his escape on his own, but little did he know that a family would lead him to Jesus but also have another plan for him, as well. We see the children at the orphanage and how God's love transforms their lives. We also see how the lives of the children intertwine, along with the staff of the orphanage. Missionaries at the orphanage lead several of the children and staff to Christ, and they care deeply for the children who, due to various circumstances, are without their parents and ended up at the orphanage.

God has not forgotten anyone. He is guiding our lives through various situations, and He has promised to be with us when we choose to follow Him.

Chapter 1. Planting the Seed of God's Word

"How then shall they call on Him in whom they have not believed? And how shall they believe in Him of whom they have not heard? And how shall they hear without a preacher?" (Romans 10:14)

It was Saturday afternoon, and the children were playing outside...all one hundred children in a big green courtyard. It was springtime, and the trees were blooming. Nature was changing into a beautiful, colorful picture, designed by the great Creator, God. It was splendid outside, and very sunny.

"Children, come to eat! Lunch is ready!" said Martha, the children's supervisor to the children.

They had almost no reaction to her call. Martha had to insist a few times until all the children were in. It was a huge room with twenty tables that had five chairs each, specially designed for them, where all the children could eat. It wasn't the nicest place, but it was much better than being on the streets. The people that worked there didn't behave with them very well, but because they got some checkups once in a while, randomly, they tried to be cautious and not misbehave. If the children didn't obey the staff, they were punished, and the level of punishment depended on what they did.

The children had to learn to be thankful for where they were and what they had, even though many of them had many questions about their lives – who their parents were and why they were abandoned. Living in the orphanage in the city of Bramka, in the country of Graceland, made some of them feel inferior to other children, but there were children among them who also knew to be thankful for what they had.

All these kids had different and very unique stories, but with the same result – they ended up in this state orphanage because their parents did not take care of them for various reasons. James, a seven-year-old boy, was left by his mom at the hospital right after giving birth to him, and he ended up as a tiny baby in the orphanage. He had survived in hard conditions, as the staff was not prepared with all the necessary facilities needed to take care of him properly. Other children, like Tommy, Fred, Kathy, Brenda, and Jessie, were left by their parents on the streets and didn't take care of them anymore. Each child was found by a social worker and taken to the orphanage after he or she was living alone on the streets, begging for food, and trying to survive another day without their parents' care. Other children, like Matt and Karen, were brought by their parents to the orphanage because they were families were impoverished and could barely make it day by day. The parents just gave them up, as they couldn't handle their situation anymore. There were many different stories that each child had, but they all had in common a hard past and a future that they weren't sure about.

As Martha gathered all the children for lunch at 1 pm, they all ate very fast, as they had special guests coming in just a few minutes, and they were so excited about it. There was a group of missionaries from the city of Keranda in the country of Ropyland, and they traveled to the city of Bramka, in the country of Graceland, where they had their mission field. Along with some other mission activities, this group of missionaries had decided to come and witness to the children in this orphanage, which was named the Looking Ahead Orphanage. The children were so excited, and they were eagerly anticipating their visit with much enthusiasm. The team came each Saturday to see these children for a few hours. They had done so for almost 3 months already. These missionaries were so happy that in the country of Graceland there was a freedom to witness with no persecution, and they were doing God's work with a lot of enthusiasm, working hard to gain people for Christ.

When these missionaries arrived, they went in the dining room, where the children were still eating. "Hi everyone, great to see you all today," said the three missionaries to these children.

"Hi! Come sit next to me," the children responded like in a choir.

The missionaries brought some sweets that the children enjoyed very much as a delicious dessert for them after lunch. They had a small box of chocolate-covered raisins for each of them.

"Thank you!" the children said with gladness that someone from outside of the orphanage was caring about them.

"You're very welcome!" the missionaries affirmed, as they were happily giving them these sweets.

"We are so glad that you came," Susan, a five years old girl said to them. "I missed you already. I wish you could come and see us every day!"

"We are so glad to be here," said Esther, Joshua, and Jonathan; the three missionaries.

"Can you go and search for my parents?" Jason, an eleven-year-old boy, exclaimed. "I really would like to meet them. I don't know who they are," he said, as he approached Esther.

Esther felt so sorry for him, and she tried to comfort him and told him about God, and the fact that God can be his Father if he believes in Christ Jesus, God's Son, and accepts the gift of salvation that is free for anyone who chooses God for his life. Esther had a long conversation with Jason and explained to him how he can become the child of God. Jason listened to her very carefully with a lot of interest. He realized that, though he much wanted to meet his parents, God could fill the empty space that had been left in his heart.

While the other children spent time together, doing a lot of outdoor activities with Jonathan and Joshua (organizing a volleyball game especially for girls, and soccer for boys, plus many other games as well), Esther was still talking to Jason and testifying God to him. To her surprise, Jason seemed to be very open about these things and accepted Christ in his life to be his Lord and Savior.

Esther helped him to pray, and he happily repeated after her the prayer:

"Dear Jesus, I know that I am a sinner and that I need you in my life. Please forgive me of all my sins and cleanse me through your blood. I accept you to be my Lord and my Savior. I want to commit to following you with faithfulness in my entire life and thank you that you will help me to do so by your grace. I trust my life in your hands and thank you that you are in control. Thank you, Heavenly Father, for accepting me as your child through Jesus. You deserve all the glory. In Jesus' name I pray. Amen."

"What a victory for God's kingdom," Esther was thinking happily and was so much looking forward to sharing with Joshua and Jonathan what just happened. She let Jason play on one of the volleyball teams, and she immediately told Joshua, her big brother, what had just happened. Joshua was so happy for Jason. He already started to think about what he could do to strengthen and encourage Jason on his path with God and focus a little bit more on discipleship with him, as Jason was the first child who came to Christ from among these children. Later on, Jonathan, their mission co-worker, found out as well, and he was excited, as well, for Jason.

While they were continuing to play games outside, the missionaries felt so sorry for James, who didn't really want to cooperate with them. He was still very affected by the fact that he found out that he had been abandoned in the hospital, and he wasn't very open to talking with other children or adults. Otherwise, he was very smart and ingenious but sometimes gave the staff a hard time, as he liked to fight with other children and make them fear him. Even though he was just seven years old, he caused a lot of trouble in the orphanage. One of the staff members even had to go to the hospital because of an accidental injury James caused. They punished him often because of his misbehavior, and he wasn't allowed to go out and play with other children during his punishment. He liked drawing, so finding something to do inside while being punished wasn't too hard for him. He showed creativity and a lot of ambition through his drawings. The staff even took one of his drawings and put it on the front door of the Looking Ahead Orphanage. James was noticed by his art teacher at the school, and his teacher was willing to give him extra hours, for free, just to help him improve his drawing skills.

After playing a lot of games for about two hours, the missionaries gathered all of them and had a few children's worship songs that they really enjoyed, and then Esther shared a Bible lesson to them. It was the parable of the lost sheep. Esther explained to the children that this lost sheep was so valuable to the shepherd that, even though he had the other ninety-nine with him, he cared so much about the lost sheep that he went to find it. She emphasized the joy that the shepherd had once he found the sheep that had been lost. He was delighted and rejoiced, as he cared so much for every sheep that he had so much that he didn't want to lose any of them. Esther told them that there is so much joy in Heaven for each person who is lost and gets saved. She explained what it means to be lost, separated from God, and that to live our life according to our own plans, not according to God's plan and purpose, is not what is best for our lives. She explained that we are all sinners and that, because of our sins, we are separated from God, and that only through Jesus Christ we can be saved. Kathy, one of the children, said:

"What is sin?"

"Sin is when you lie, steal, quarrel, don't love your neighbor and do all sorts of bad things," Esther explained to her.

"Does God still love us when we sin?" asked Bob, a nine years old boy.

"Yes, Bob! God loves us still, and He wants to wash our sins through Christ's blood. This is possible when we come before God and are sorry for what we did wrong. God forgives us and gives us grace."

"What is grace?" another child asked.

"Grace is to receive an undeserved gift. God's salvation is by grace because we all deserved the sentence of death, but we can all have life through Jesus Christ if we believe in Him and repent," Esther said.

Many questions came one after the other, and many children were very interested in this subject. Along with the children, two adults that were part of the orphanage staff had questions as well, Martha and Samantha.

As there were so many questions and a lot of interaction, Joshua and Jonathan were also helping

Esther respond to them. They were all glad by the openness of these children.

The children were paying a lot of attention, except for James, who didn't really seem to fit in so well. He was too busy playing with his stuffed toy bear and paying attention to him a lot. James liked his bear so much, and he named him "Buddy," as he considered him his best friend that was there for him. He very rarely was seen without his bear. He got him as a Christmas present three years ago, and he was still so attached to him. Even though he didn't talk to other people so much, you could sometimes see him talking alone with his Buddy. He considered Buddy part of his family, and since he didn't really understand why he was abandoned in the hospital by his mom, he was determined not to abandon Buddy and was closely taking care of him.

After responding to some more questions, the missionaries sang a Christian song entitled *Come to Christ*. The verses of it were very profound, and the first verse was like this:

"God wants you to be saved
Just come to Christ
And listen to His Word
He will show you the path

And lost you will be no more
If you believe and repent."

After this song, Jonathan who was leading it by playing his guitar said to the children, "If you want to give your life to Christ, and live for His glory, then have the courage to come in front near us and let us pray for you."

Kathy, Bob, and Matt stepped out in the front of the room. They gave their lives to Jesus; Esther, Jonathan, and Joshua prayed with them. To their surprise, Martha the young lady, who was there as the orphanage staff, stepped out in the front of the room as well and dedicated her life to Jesus right there, and Joshua helped her pray to God.

"Wow, what a beautiful day! God has worked in such a wonderful way and called so many people to follow him today," the missionaries thought as they were on their way home from the orphanage. They thought about Jason, Kathy, Bob, Matt, and Martha.

They were very thankful that Martha opened up about her heart for God. This way, as a Christian adult among these children, she could tell them more about Christ and be a witness in the orphanage even in those days that the missionaries weren't there. They felt very blessed by God that He used them in that orphanage in such a wonderful way. They were very encouraged that, after going week after week there for about three months already, God did great things that day.

At the orphanage, the children were having dinner - one of their favorite foods, homemade pizza. They enjoyed it so much!

Even though James wasn't too talkative with many people, he was a good friend of Jason who had just gotten saved. In the evening, Jason shared his experience with James:

"Hey James, I have some great news to tell you!"
"What is it, Jason?"

"You won't believe this, but I'm God's child now. It is such a good feeling to know that I have a Heavenly Father who takes care of me."

"Hmmm... how is that possible?"

"It is a free gift, as Jesus paid instead of me the price for my salvation – on the cross, and He washed away all my sins through His blood on the cross. You can be saved as well, God loves you so much." Jason was talking with so much confidence and joy in his heart.

"Thanks, Jason, for telling me! I'm busy now; I want to finish this drawing..." He didn't know what to tell Jason to leave him alone... especially because he was planning an escape from the orphanage and he thought that if he leaves the orphanage and be on his own outside of the orphanage gates, he will have a better life.

James didn't like the high-security level that the orphanage had. As he was more rebellious, he was planning an escape, as he didn't like feeling like he was in prison. Besides school and planned outside activities once in a while, the children didn't go out often, especially by themselves. He knew that a trip to a well-known zoo from the city of Providence, around 200 miles away from Bramka, was about to come. He wanted to escape to a different city, where nobody knew him. At the age of seven, this is what he thought would bring him happiness.

Chapter 2. An Answered Prayer

"And whatever things you ask in prayer, believing, you will receive" (Matthew 21:22).

The Looking Ahead Orphanage was supported by the state; therefore, the financial resources were not overwhelming. However, with adequate resource management, things were good. Occasionally, some people gave money to support the orphanage's cause, and that was very helpful. Salaries were low at this orphanage; therefore, staff turnover was very high because many staff members found higher paying jobs and chose the money over the value of the job's impact. If a child somehow got attached to someone from the staff emotionally, they had to learn how to detach as soon as that person left the organization. This made it hard for the children since they didn't have parents to take care of them and the staff was not so stable.

Martha, the young lady who gave her life to Christ on Saturday, was well appreciated by the staff leadership because she was already with them for 5 years, which was a record for the orphanage staff, and she was dedicated to her job, as the children's supervisor. One day, Roger, the orphanage director, wanted to give her a great news.

"Hey, Martha! How are you?" Roger approached her.

"I'm good, Roger, thank you for asking! And you?"

"I'm also good! I just wanted to thank you for being very faithful to your work at this orphanage. As a sign of appreciation for serving here for 5 years already, you will get support to go and study at the State University of Bramka. You can go and get your Marketing degree that you were hoping for, if this is still your dream."

"Oh, wow! That is amazing! That is indeed my dream! Thank you so much! Praise the Lord!"

"So, you can get ready to start this fall!"
"I sure will!"

"I hope you will manage to do both your Bachelor's degree and work here at the same time, as the children care a lot about you and would want to see you around."

"No worries, I'm sure I can do both, by God's grace! He will give me strength!"

Martha got such excellent news, and she was very pleased about it! She finally had the chance to go and meet her dream of having a Bachelor's degree in Marketing. She was amazed how fast God answered her prayer. She became a Christian on Saturday, and here it comes, this big news on Monday. Wow, she was amazed! She went to a remote area and gave thanks to God for this amazing thing He did for her! She wanted to go and study and develop her professional skills more, but she couldn't afford it, financially; now God had provided. She was very thankful and was thinking that maybe one day she could promote the orphanage and make it more known to people so that whoever wants to support these children or even adopt one of them could more easily do so.

Up until now, only Elisabeth, Klara, Jay and Louis had been adopted by different families, from what Martha knew. She thought that more children could get that chance and, if more couples would see how wonderful these children are and be ready to invest in them and give them a proper home and the love and harmony they could get only in a family environment, many lives could be changed this way. She was hoping that this Marketing degree will benefit the orphanage a lot.

As a general rule, the orphanage was open for families who wanted to adopt children. Out of those one hundred children they had, the range of ages was between 4 and 16 years old. They had some babies as well, just like James had been when he arrived, who got to the orphanage just a few days after being born and who had been abandoned in the hospital. Some married couples came and visited Looking Ahead Orphanage, and a few children were placed into happy families over the years. In order to keep the number the same, one hundred children, the orphanage took other children in the adopted children's place. One hundred children was the maximum capacity of the orphanage, and the leaders liked to keep up that number so that they could offer help to the largest number of children they could afford to help.

Once a child was placed in a family, the other children missed that child but also wondered why they were not chosen. And after several adoptions from the orphanage, the children left behind kept wondering why they could not be part of a family and have nice parents to take care of them. James was among those children who wanted a family so much; he didn't like the orphanage environment and was just hoping that one day he will be the chosen child by a married couple so that he would finally have a nice family to live in. However, that day hadn't come for him yet, and he was just dreaming about the day he would be adopted.

Chapter 3. Planning the Trip to the Zoo

"Every good gift and every perfect gift is from above, and comes down from the Father of lights, with whom there is no variation or shadow of turning" (James 1:17).

The Looking Ahead Orphanage leadership planned a very nice trip to a famous zoo from the city of Providence. They very rarely had outings scheduled for these children, usually once per year, for Children's Day, which was right on April 2nd in Graceland country. It was a very special national holiday, and many parents did great things for their children that day.

Since it was such a special day in Graceland, it was a national holiday so parents could spend more time with their children. As in any other national holiday, some businesses were still open and made lots of profits because many other businesses were closed. Usually, the places most likely to be open were the ones where children went, such as the zoo, for instance.

Because the Looking Ahead orphans' parents were not there, someone else had to make that day special for them. The children felt special, and they were being treated specially for April 2nd.

Usually, many of the children realize during this type of celebration how much they miss having parents, especially when seeing other children with their parents, very happy and smiling, showing the joy that is overflowing from their hearts. They wished they could be like that as well, not trapped in an orphanage where some times were good, but other times it felt as if no one cared. It was that feeling of being important once in a while to the staff, as on Children's Day, but so many other days feeling abandoned and missing being a part of a happy and nice family.

Children's Day was on a Wednesday, and the children didn't have to go to school either so they could celebrate the National Day dedicated to children.

The orphanage staff met with all one hundred children Monday evening and reminded them of the trip they would have on Wednesday. All the children were gathered together and were listening to instructions:

"Martha, Samantha, and Joe will be going with you on Wednesday! Please listen to them!" said Roger, the orphanage director, to the children.

"I will not be able to go with you this time, but I hope you will have a great time together at the zoo, and you will all have a nice surprise waiting for you when you have breakfast on Wednesday morning before you leave," he continued.

"What surprise?" a girl asked him, very curious as to what it could be.

"You will find out on Wednesday! I'm sure you will like it!"

"Hurray!" some children exclaimed as they were excited about Wednesday.

"Also, be very careful how you behave on the bus! Samantha, Martha, and Joe will be there with you the whole time. Please listen to them! I honestly hope no one will misbehave. Otherwise, there will be consequences! Now, go to your rooms."

On the way out, many children were very happy about Wednesday, among which was Jason, who was praising God and was saying out loud:

"Thank you, God! You are wonderful!"

Kathy, Bob, and Matt were also very happy about what will happen on Wednesday. They learned how to be thankful, and the missionaries also encouraged the children that accepted Christ in their hearts and discipled them more, allowing them to continue to grow spiritually.

Even though Roger wasn't a Christian, at the missionaries' permission, he let Jason, Kathy, Bob, and Matt go with them to Church on Sunday. Esther, Joshua, and Jonathan were responsible for them and took care of them. They went to pick up these children, brought them to Church with them, and then brought them back afterward. They wished they could take all of the children with them, but Roger allowed them to take only these for now. Martha, the children's supervisor, also went with them to Church on Sundays when she was off work.

It was nice that they could go to Church, and they even made new friends among Christian children at Church. They really liked it. All of them received a Bible from Church, as a gift, and they loved reading it at the orphanage. They could all read, as they were already going to school for a few years. Jason was in the fifth grade, Katha was in the third grade, Bob was in the fourth grade, and Matt was in the seventh grade. Sometimes, when they were reading the Bible at the orphanage, the other children saw them, and they could testify God to them as well, particularly through this way.

Jason, Kathy, Bob, and Matt were planned to take their Bibles with them on Wednesday. James planned to take Buddy with him, as he did very often. He went to school, as well, with Buddy, as he was in the first grade.

Because Jason and James were the best of friends, Jason sometimes read to James from the Bible, hoping that he would understand as well and that, one day, he would accept Jesus as his Savior. Jason also read the story that Esther told them one time, the parable of the lost sheep. James paid more attention this time to it. He thought about what would happen if he couldn't find Buddy anymore. He was happy that the shepherd found the lost sheep.

Chapter 4. Going to the Zoo

"The heavens declare the glory of God; And the firmament shows His handiwork" (Psalm 19:1).

It was 7 a.m. on Wednesday morning. The children had just woken up, and they knew that it is going to be a very special day, although not everyone was anticipating it as much or was so happy about it. The good thing is that the majority of them were happy about it.

"Children, wake up! Get ready to come and eat your breakfast!" Samantha said to them.

"It is going to be a wonderful day!" Martha added.

"Hurray!" many children said, while others were hardly getting up still.

James had his own plans in place to escape on this particular day. Even though the leadership planned a nice day for the children, James planned an escape from the orphanage environment, as he wanted to be free from the orphanage. However, he did not know what was waiting for him. He thought that he would live a better life away from so many rules and be able to do what he wants. At only seven years old, this was his plan, but God had an even better plan for him, one that he could not have anticipated, even though planning his escape was wrong.

The children went to breakfast, and as promised by Roger, the orphanage director, they found a nice surprise there. Along with pizza for breakfast, that they all enjoyed, each got a bag with many sweets inside: different types of chocolate and candies. They were all delighted. They also got some snacks and sandwiches for taking with them on the trip.

Soon after breakfast, the staff gathered the children and got ready for a big day. The private bus the orphanage leadership team had arranged for them was there with a driver that was available for them that entire day. All one hundred children went on the bus, along with Samantha, Martha and Joe, their supervisors.

They had some nice children songs on the bus at the request of Roger, the orphanage director. One of the songs was like this:

"Oh, children, be joyful
Today is very special
Just enjoy the sun and play

This is a special day..."

Providence, where the zoo was, was two hundred miles away by bus. It took about 4 hours of driving by bus to get there from Bramka. Between Bramka and Providence cities, the view was splendid and especially from the bus so much could be seen already.

The sky was a very light blue with just a few almost transparent clouds on it. It was very sunny and beautiful out there. The children didn't go on trips like this one too often, so many of them were amazed at God's handiwork. It was so amazing! Martha, Samantha, and Joe were also very glad that it was such a beautiful day for Children's Day. They were also glad that the children were not very loud and they seemed to cope well with them.

Some of the children were singing along with the music they heard on the bus. It was a friendly atmosphere for them, and they enjoyed the children's songs.

James didn't forget his bear. He was very nervous as well for what was going to happen next. Instead of being very joyful, as many of the other children were, he chose to be discontent, even on this nice day. Instead of being happy, he chose to be sad. He didn't even notice how beautiful the world was outside.

He was just trying to be indifferent and finalize his plan of escape. As they get there, he would be with the children almost until the end of the zoo visit, and almost before getting out of the zoo, he would hide and stay a little bit longer at the zoo and then find his own way in Providence. He was actually glad that he was further away from Bramka so that he couldn't easily be found.

In James' mind, he thought that this was an excellent opportunity to start his life on his own, to take care of himself, and to do what he wants. He had a few sheets of paper and the tools he needed to draw, and he planned to keep drawing and eventually sell his drawings and make a living out of it. He also had Buddy with him, so that gave him more courage to take on his plan to escape as he didn't feel alone especially when he was around him. He knew he might miss some of the things from the orphanage, especially Jason, but he was ready to give up even their friendship to pursue his plan. In his heart, he also hoped to find someone who would adopt him. Sadly, he didn't tell anyone about it, and everything was based on his own thoughts and no outside advice. Probably if he would have discussed things more openly, then things would have been different, and the orphanage staff would have taken some steps to help him in meeting his emotional needs better.

Between Bramka and Providence, the driver stopped the bus twice so that the children could take some short breaks for going to the bathroom and for eating some of their snacks and food they had with them.

Each time the bus stopped, people looked astonished, as there were so many children at once, but they thought that maybe a special event is happening for Children's Day and parents let their children go together on an organized trip. They didn't think that these children might be coming from an orphanage because these children were pretty respectful and had good manners, at least most of them.

After about four hours, they finally got to the zoo.

"Here we are! How is everyone?" Joe asked the children.

"Hurray! We arrived!" some children said, as a reply.

"Fine!" "Good!" "Excited!" other children exclaimed, in a chorus.

They went out from the bus, as the driver, Mark, parked the bus near the zoo. He went with them inside. Joe bought tickets for the entire group, as he had gotten the money from Roger, and he was responsible for the financial things for this trip. As he got tickets for everyone, they were allowed to enter. It was already 1:23 p.m., as Joe was looking to see what time it was.

"Come, children, let's go in and explore the beauty of the zoo!" Joe said.

"Oh, wow! Look at that baby monkey, how he is pointing to us with his hand." Martha remarked.

"Maybe he wants some food!" Jason added.

"Well, unfortunately, we cannot give them any food! Look what the sign says – 'Don't feed the animals'!"

As they went on, they could see different types of birds, fish, snakes, crocodiles, giraffes, kangaroos, elephants, etc.

When they got to see the elephants, one of the elephants was drinking water. The elephant had a pool of water right in front of it and started drinking. It took water in through its trunk and then put its trunk in its mouth afterward. It did this a few times and took in a large amount of water overall.

"Wow, he drank so much water! That is amazing!" Tommy and Jessie observed as they were carefully paying a lot of attention to them.

They spent most of their time at the zoo in front of the elephants and were astonished. They really liked these two elephants. It was extraordinary. It was a big elephant along with a baby elephant, so they thought it was probably the baby elephant and its mommy elephant along with him.

Surprisingly, James liked the elephants, as well as other animals, though he was very isolated from the other children and wasn't given too much importance since many of the children were looking at all the amazing animals. The orphanage hadn't organized a trip to the zoo before, so, probably for every child, it was their first experience at the zoo. They had seen animals like these before, either pictured in different books they had read or in movies, etc., but not up close in person, at least not all of these types.

At the bird section of the zoo, they especially noticed the parrots. Some of them were the special type, the talking parrots. Three talking parrots fascinated people who came to visit the zoo. They knew how to talk, as they were trained by specialists. One of the parrots said to the group of children:

"Hi everyone, enjoy the zoo!"

"Oh, wow! He is actually talking! That is amazing!" Jason said, very happily.

The other two talking parrots said things as well, such as:

"I love you!"
"I'm hungry!"
"Beautiful day!"
"Be happy!"
"Look at me!"

"You are great!"

"Oh, wow!" the children said amazed. They wanted to have at least a talking parrot to take with them at the orphanage and to enjoy. They really liked it there a lot.

James loved this part of the zoo a lot. He didn't know that there were such parrots that could talk. He wished that his stuffed toy bear, Buddy, could talk as well, but Buddy was just a toy and didn't make any sounds at all. Still, it was James' favorite toy.

After a long visit to the zoo and seeing such a diversity of animals, including lions and tigers, which were some of their favorites as well, and also horses, camels, even rabbits that they enjoyed, they were about to go back to their home, the orphanage.

During their visit, the children couldn't help but notice the other children who were there with their families. It was the deep desire of every child that was part of that orphanage, to belong to a family of their own, but they weren't in control of that. It wasn't their fault that they couldn't be part of a typical family, and they had to be happy with what they had.

Some days were harder at the orphanage - the children could sense that - and every child had his or her own moments of loneliness when he or she was thinking about life and how he or she was different compared to the other classmates at school.

Other times, the orphanage staff wasn't too friendly with these children. They sometimes saw what they had to do as just a job they got paid for doing and didn't always care so much about it, especially because of the meager pay for which the orphanage was known. The staff wasn't too dedicated always, and the children knew that. Still, it wasn't them that could change something. Also, if they got too attached by some of the staff, they would leave after a short time, when they would get a better job for themselves and the children would miss them a lot. The children had many hard moments at the orphanage, and many of these were based on emotional needs that only real parents could meet. They were still not completely understanding why they must be different from the rest of the children they knew from school and why they couldn't have what they have. They sometimes could not understand their classmates that had families, when they didn't value what they had but just took their families for granted, as if they deserved to have a loving mom, dad, and siblings.

James had his very deep feelings as well, and he chose for his life in his mind. He would go and live his life on his own, and also one of his more deeper thoughts was to try and find himself a good mom and dad. He wanted so much to be adopted and, when he saw other children that were adopted from the orphanage, he wished for himself to be in that same category. However, it didn't happen yet, and in his mind, he thought that, maybe, in his freedom, he could somehow find a mom or a dad for himself, someone who would adopt and love him. By that time, he was convinced that he could make a living on his own.

While all the children were still looking at the lions and how they were roaring, James thought about isolating himself from the group, little by little, and hiding. Samantha, Martha, and Joe didn't even notice as they were all so engaged with the visit to the lions and until now everything seemed to be fine, so they weren't looking constantly at all the children. James managed to hide behind a bush that was close by. After the group had gone on towards the exit of the zoo, James went on the opposite way to get further back in the zoo.

Everyone was exhausted, and it was already around 6 p.m. by the time they went to the bus. Because there were so many children, they didn't notice that one was missing. They failed to count them all, as they did when they left from Bramka, and because of the supervisors' mistake, James was no longer with them. James wasn't too talkative anyway, so it was hard to figure out that he was missing. The driver went on and drove back to the orphanage. Most of the children fell asleep on their way back, as well as the supervisors. The music on the bus wasn't on anymore so that everyone who wanted could rest in silence.

When they got back to Bramka, the supervisors who were with the children, Samantha, Martha, and Joe, left the children at the orphanage for the night shift staff, and they went on back to their homes. Everyone was exhausted...

Chapter 5. Someone Is Missing

"Where can I go from your Spirit? Or where can I flee from Your presence?"
(Psalm 139:7)

After they arrived at the orphanage, and after Samantha, Martha, and Joe already left, Emma, the night shift supervisor, had a thought that she should count the children. She didn't know why she had this though, and she didn't think anyone would be missing anyway, but she still decided to count them. As she was counting, instead of one hundred, she found only ninety-nine children. She thought it was just a counting mistake, so she counted them again. And, to her surprise, the result was the same. Still, ninety-nine children. She was getting alarmed, so she counted them again and again.

"No way! Someone is missing!" Emma exclaimed loudly.

"Someone is missing?" Rebecca, a fourteen years old girl said.

"Yes, Rebecca, that is correct!"

"Who could be missing?" Sam, a twelve years old boy said as he was surprised.

"I'm not sure!" Emma said.

"Children, please look around and try to figure out who is not here with us now!" she continued.

After a few minutes, Jason was astonished:
"Oh, no, James is no longer here!"

"James, James! Are you here somewhere?" Emma and some of the children started to scream out loud to try and find him.

There was no answer.

Alarmed, Emma called Martha:
"Hi, Martha! We have an emergency!"

"Hi! What is it, Emma?"

"I don't know how this is possible, but you only brought back ninety-nine children! We found out who is missing – James!"

"Oh, no! That is not good at all!" Martha exclaimed.

Martha remembered that they didn't count the children before they left the zoo. She felt so sorry for that huge mistake, and she was thinking how was this possible, not to think about counting the children and leaving like that.

Because she was a Christian, and because this was already out of her control, she trusted James in God's hands, that He would be with him. She bowed down and, on her knees, she prayed with tears in her eyes:

"Dear Heavenly Father,

Please forgive me, and Joe and Samantha as well, for not being so responsible for all one hundred children that were entrusted to us and leaving one of them in Providence. I pray that You will protect James as he is there on his own. Please don't let anything happen to him, and may Your protection be over him. I pray that, in Your grace, You will help us to find him and bring him back here to take care of him. Please help him, and give him wisdom and may Your presence be with him. I trust him deeply in Your mighty hands, and I thank You that You will provide. May Your Name be honored.

In Jesus' Name I pray,

Amen."

Chapter 6. Following His Own Plan

"Look at the birds of the air, for they neither sow nor reap nor gather into barns; yet your heavenly Father feeds them. Are you not of more value than they?" (Matthew 6:26)

James followed his own plan of escape and succeeded. He felt happy, at first, for what he did, thinking that this way he would be happier than at orphanage and that he could enjoy his life of freedom, not being limited by strict rules that the orphanage imposed. But as he was wandering around alone at the zoo, with his toy bear in his arms, he started to feel sorry for his decision.

He began to miss Jason, his good friend and, strangely, he started to miss what he had at the orphanage, especially as time went by. He was thinking more about what he had at the orphanage and took for granted rather than being thankful. He realized how much he had at the orphanage, compared to how little he had now... almost nothing. Why did he have to take the hard step of leaving the orphanage? What led him to it?

It was getting darker, and he was still inside the zoo... As he kept thinking about it, as he had plenty of time to think, he started crying and feeling very sorry for what he did. He just wanted to be again in his bed and just wake up and find out that all this was just a nightmare, but unfortunately, it was so real, and he had done this to himself.

He planned his escape very carefully and succeeded, but he didn't think too much about all the details of what he would need to do next. Also, he didn't think about the fact that he had no money with him to go back to the Looking Ahead Orphanage and say that he was so sorry for what he did.

While Martha was praying for him at around 10:30 pm on that day, April 2nd, James felt comforted but didn't know why. God was with him, even though James didn't know why he felt more secure. He stopped crying after almost an entire hour...

He was exhausted and felt hungry as well. As he looked in his book bag, he realized he still had a sandwich, a little bit more water left in his bottle and a lot of sweets with him. He ate the sandwich very fast as he was very hungry and he got some more strength. The zoo staff didn't notice that anyone was inside the zoo still, as each time James saw someone coming towards him, he hid ahead of time, so he remained unnoticed.

It was a hard evening for him, especially as it was getting dark and he could hear the lions roar and all kinds of animals making different sounds. He felt trapped in the middle of the jungle. Thinking about the fact that all these animals were captive, he felt more secure, but still, he didn't truly enjoy the frightening atmosphere by himself. As it was already 11 pm and was sitting on a bench inside the zoo, he lay down and fell asleep.

In the morning, he was awakened by the sounds of the animals and by the sun, which was rising so nicely. He enjoyed the beauty of it, and he got up. He realized that he is still in the middle of the zoo and it was still not just a dream.

James was very hungry, and he thought about eating something, but looking in his book bag, he noticed that he only had some sweets left. He devoured them, but he was still hungry for some real food. He again thought back to his breakfasts at the orphanage, and how well all the children must be eating right now.

Usually, they had good meals, not too abundant or too diverse, but enough to not be hungry and have a pretty healthy diet. The orphanage staff tried to manage the limited resources they had as well as they could and at the same time invest in the children's diet and not let them starve, which James was now thankful for. He looked back at how many times he was served the meals and had a terrible attitude, and not even caring too much about it, just eating what was served without gratitude. He wished now he could be there and not feel the hunger that he was now facing.

He was a little bit afraid, as he was alone. He started talking to Buddy:

"Oh, my dear Buddy. What did I do? We are here, and I don't know what to do now. I miss the orphanage so much. I'm sorry that I planned this escape, and I just now realize how bad my thought was to escape. At least I had a bed in which to sleep, food provided, I could go to school... and also, it was nice to have Esther, Jonathan, and Joshua coming over on Saturdays, even though I didn't know how to appreciate all these things."

Then he started thinking about the lost sheep from the Bible... how Esther was explaining this but he didn't really pay too much attention. He understood more when Jason read it for him from the Bible, and now he understood that he is like the lost sheep. He felt afraid, lonely, and separated from all the other ninety-nine children that were well taken care of at the orphanage.

He was hoping that someone would come and search for him. He wanted to be rescued from his condition and taken care of. He thought in his mind that, if someone would have mercy on him, and would again somehow get back to the orphanage or even better in a nice family, he would definitely appreciate everything he had and would choose to live a life of gratitude and thankfulness.

He had some paper with him and tools to draw, so he started drawing, hoping to sell what he drew. It took him about two hours to draw something. It was the orphanage in Bramka that he missed so much. He drew the landscape around it as well.

What should he do now? He was starving, so he needed something to eat. He went out from the zoo, as the gate was open now, and started trying to sell his drawing. It was indeed a very nice drawing that he made, and he was very talented. He walked on the streets and asked people to buy the drawing.

Many people passed by him with no interest at all, as they were busy with their own lives.

Providence was much bigger than Bramka, it had three times more people. Providence was a well-known city, and many rich people lived there. It was known for having the highest standard of living. Everything was very nice in Providence: nice buildings, different points of attraction that brought many tourists in the area, many successful businesses, and more people from the higher class than in the average city.

Security was also high in Providence, as police officers tried to maintain a peaceful environment to protect this area. Because much wealth was found in this city, it was a point of attraction for thieves and burglars who wanted to have what others had without having to make too much effort.

James felt discouraged. After about three hours of trying to sell his drawing, he felt he didn't have the strength anymore. He just lay down on the ground in front of a very agglomerated marketplace. A poor elderly lady noticed him, looked at the drawing, and liked it a lot. She asked James:

"Is this drawing for sale?" she asked.

"Yes, it is! Would you please buy it? I'm so hungry, and I would like to go and buy some food for myself."

She came to the marketplace herself to sell two pounds of carrots and two pounds of apples. This is all that she had for sale, and she was making a hard living.

Her husband was at home and very sick, so she had to manage each day to carry something from her courtyard to the marketplace and try to sell that. She grew some vegetables, but it was hard for her to carry too much as she couldn't afford to take the bus to the marketplace. They lived day by day, very hard. Still, she felt very sorry for this little boy she had in front of her now.

"Come with me," she said to him.

James obeyed her. She went to a spring, washed two apples, and handed them to James. She said, "You can have these and eat them," hoping that he will get some strength.

James was so thankful, and he said: "Thank you so much! You are very kind to me!"

"I'm glad I could help you some!"

After he had eaten the apples, she confessed to him that besides the two pounds of apples she had for sale, those two apples were all that she had for lunch, so James realized that this very nice lady gave up all that she had to eat for lunch so that he could have food. "Wow, she was truly very kind," he thought to himself.

Because of what she did for him, and because he knew that she likes the drawing he did so much, he said: "I would like for you to have this drawing. I noticed that you like it a lot! I want to make it a gift to you!"

"Wow, that is lovely! It is very kind of you!" the elderly woman said.

She looked in her pocket to see if she had some money and she found four quarters. She handed those to James, saying:

"This is not much, but it is all I have with me now. Take this, and I hope this will be useful to you in some way!"

"Thank you so much! You have done so much for me today!" James replied.

As they said bye to each other, James went on. Not long after, he ran across a man who was selling warm croissants with cheese at a special discounted price for that particular day: three for one dollar.

James had one dollar from the elderly lady, and he bought three croissants for himself. He ate two and kept one for later, as he wasn't sure what was going to happen to him later, and he knew he might be again hungry.

He stopped in a very nice park, and, as it was spring, it was splendid outside. It was around 4 pm, and he took his stuffed bear closer to him and sat down on a bench. He was already very tired as he walked so much on the streets. He was amazed how hard it was to sell the drawing and how busy people were when they passed by him. Many didn't even notice him, he thought. He was still thinking about the elderly woman, and he was very thankful for what she had done for him that day.

He had a few more pieces of paper and started to draw some more, hoping that people will buy more of his drawings. He was thinking to make enough money to take the bus to Bramka and go back to the orphanage. The ticket would cost him twenty-five dollars. Based on how it had gone today so far, he had little hope that he would soon return to the orphanage. Also, the city was so big, and he didn't even know exactly where the bus station was to go back to Bramka. He was so confused about many things.

He continued drawing on a piece of paper. This time, he drew two beautiful apples, as he kept thinking about them. On the bottom-left corner of the paper, he also drew two coins. This drawing represented a very nice experience for him, for which he was very thankful.

Looking around, as he was drawing, he noticed many children in that park. Some were happy, other ones sad. He always thought that children that have parents and live in a normal family are always happy. He didn't think that even with their parents next to them, other children could be so sad.

“I want that doll from the store!” a little girl screamed to her mom, as she passed by James. She screamed that several times, out loud, and was very much wanting ice cream. Her mom didn’t know how to stop her from crying, and she already was all red on her face from so much embarrassment.

Her mom said to her: “Let’s go home, you have enough dolls already!”
“No, I want that one that I just saw! Buy it for me! I want it now!” the girl said to her mom.

James was completely shocked. He looked at his toy bear, and he thought about how many toys he had. He realized that Buddy the bear was his only toy, and he kept it very close to him. He had some other toys that he rarely got, and he couldn’t really choose what he wanted to get. Also, he had to share his toys with the other children at the orphanage as well, so after a while, he just remained with his stuffed bear. All the other toys had vanished, and he didn’t even realize what happened to them or where they had gotten lost. Still, he was so happy about Buddy, and he cared about this precious toy a lot.

James also realized that he didn't really need many other toys for him to be happy. What he thought he needs to be happy was to be part of a real family. Still, being alone as he was now made him appreciate the orphanage so much and realize that there was his true home. He understood how much he had, and he missed that a lot.

He finished his drawing with the two apples and the two coins on it, and then he started going up to people in the park to try to sell the drawing.

James was a very sweet boy, very calm and patient, and he didn't usually talk a lot, but when he talked he had a very soft voice. He sometimes made problems for the orphanage staff in Bramka, but that was because of the bad attitude he had towards things, as he didn't appreciate what he had.

Five mothers were letting their children play together in the park. James went to the mothers and asked them if they would like to buy the drawing. The ladies looked at him and then at the drawing and truly liked the drawing. They wanted to know if he was the one who drew it.

"Yes, I drew it! I'm passionate about drawing!" James replied.

"I'm sure my husband would like this a lot! He owns an art studio!" one of the ladies said.

"How much does it cost?" she continued.

"Five dollars!" James replied.

"I will buy it, and I will give it to my husband as a gift! He has an art collection, and I'm sure he would love this!" James said thank you to the lady that gave him the money, and he was full of gratitude in his heart. He knew how much he needed money to buy something to drink and eat.

After he had gotten the money from the lady, he went to the grocery store right across the park. He wanted to buy some water and maybe some snacks. He didn't really know how the prices are there and how much he would have to pay for things at the store. To his surprise, things were costly. He could buy only a bottle of water and one sandwich. The total amount was four dollars and seventy cents. He was amazed, as he thought how expensive everything was in the store.

He thought to himself that he had to sell the drawings at a higher price. He thought that ten dollars would be a better price.

He went back to the park, ate the sandwich, and drank some water. He continued to draw and, while sitting on the bench, he drew on three more pieces of paper. On one piece of paper, he drew a very nice sunshine, on another one he drew his Buddy bear, and on the third piece of paper he drew one of the trees he saw in the park in front of him.

After he had finished all the drawings, he was very tired. He had a long, lonely day but learned a lot. It was getting darker, but he didn't know where to go and find a shelter, so he lay down on the bench in the park where he was. He put his bookbag next to him and the drawings below it, and he held his bear in his arms and went to sleep.

While he was sleeping, an elderly man, who didn't have a shelter either and was sleeping where he could, looked at him and then noticed the book bag and the three drawings next to him. He didn't know who the child was, but, based on the clothing he had on him, the boy didn't seem to be an orphan left out on the streets. Thinking that he might find valuable things in his book bag, he took it, along with the drawings, and ran away.

In the morning, when he woke up, James found only his stuffed bear in his arms. He had nothing else, besides the thirty cents in his pocket. He was very sad and started to cry. He felt very lonely again and with no hope this time, as he didn't have his tools to draw anymore and no drawings to sell either. It was already Friday morning, April 4th.

Chapter 7. The Orphanage Alarmed

"What man of you, having a hundred sheep, if he loses one of them, does not leave the ninety-nine in the wilderness, and go after the one which is lost until he finds it?" (Luke 15:4)

On Wednesday night, April 2nd, when Emma noticed that James is missing, she was alarmed. She called Martha, who desperately prayed for him and felt very sorry for what happened. Emma also called Roger, the director of the orphanage. He was completely shocked, as he would never have expected such a thing to happen.

Roger, who was already sleeping at around 10:50 p.m. when he received the call, got up from the bed and got ready fast and went to the orphanage. He didn't want to call the authorities because he was afraid that the orphanage might suffer from this negligence and even be closed down, and the children would have to move somewhere else. He didn't know what the consequences would be, so he didn't act publicly. He tried to gather a trusted team of people that he knew so that they could go and search for James.

He asked Martha, Samantha, and Joe to go and find him in Providence after telling them that they would not have a month's salary because of negligence in work. It was already hard for them financially, so this made it extremely hard for them, but they were glad on the other side that it wasn't something worse, and they really hoped that they would find James soon.

Also, Roger went himself to try and find him. They split into two teams so that Roger went with Joe and Martha went with Samantha. They left on Thursday morning, April 3rd, at 7:30 am. It took about four hours of driving to get to Providence.

Roger, Joe, Martha, and Samantha went to the zoo first. They asked workers from there if they had seen a boy around and tried to describe what he was wearing: a blue sweater, black jeans, a brown book bag, and, the most important they thought, a stuffed toy bear in his arms. Someone among the workers remembered seeing a boy with a toy bear in his arms, and he remembered that, when he saw him walking out from the zoo, he was surprised to see him alone, without parents. That caught his attention, but he didn't say anything to him, unfortunately.

Roger and the other three had some more hope. They were convicted to go around the city and try to find him. They planned where they would go with both cars.

They went mainly by car and looked carefully on the streets of Providence. They had just very short breaks that day. After looking around on a lot of streets, they finally met later in the evening that day with no success. They had still not found James. They started to lose some hope and wondered if something bad had happened to him. They planned to look for him again the next day, and combine going by car to walking in different places where they thought he would go.

Martha was trying to encourage the team, by saying: "I've been praying for James! I'm sure that God is taking care of him, and He is in control over his life!"

"Thank you for your encouragement, Martha!" Roger said.

"I truly hope we will find him tomorrow!" Joe added.

"Yes, me too! I hope he is safe," said Samantha.

They found housing in a hotel in separate rooms, and they planned to meet in the morning and start searching again for James. Roger was thinking that he soon should alert the authorities to get more help in finding James. He cared about James a lot.

Chapter 8. A Little Boy in a Big City

"Fear not, for I am with you; Be not dismayed, for I am your God. I will strengthen you, Yes, I will help you, I will uphold you with My righteous right hand" (Isaiah 41:10).

James felt very small in such a big city. He just thought about how hard it was the other day to sell a drawing, and now he had nothing to sell. How would he make a living? What would happen to him? He didn't know what to do. He then thought about going to ask people to have mercy on him and give him food or money.

He begged on the streets, or in stores, or in restaurants. It was Friday morning, and he hadn't had breakfast yet.

He told people he randomly met: "Have mercy on me! Please give me some food or money!"

People mainly ignored him and didn't even notice him. They were busy with their own lives, with their own jobs they had to go to, etc. Many were in a hurry, so they passed by fast, others walked slowly but didn't think of him as being important to them.

He asked people for mercy for about two hours and had no response. Then, he started to cry and stop people on the streets and ask for help with anything they could. Some people pushed him away just to allow themselves to move forward with their own busy lives and with their busy schedules, too busy to stop by and listen to a child that really needed help.

Some people gave him money, to his surprise. He got some coins: someone gave him one cent, another person, five cents, and more people giving ten cents. He got about one dollar and fifty cents from people, in total. With his thirty cents that he still had in his pocket, he went to the store and bought himself a croissant and some candy and remained with no money again.

He continued to beg from people, how he could and where he could. Some felt sorry for him, and people were more open to giving in the evening when they were no longer having to run from one place to another and going on errands for themselves or for their jobs.

Some people gave him some food as well, and he was full of gratitude when that happened. He experienced different situations that particular day, from being very hungry to eating a croissant and some candies but not drinking any water. Later, he could afford to buy water. As people were giving him more money, and some food as well, he was very thankful.

He realized that his condition was not too good, and his thoughts were at the orphanage again, often, and at how much he had there.

He missed Jason and the other children surprisingly much. He felt so lonely in such a big city. He just wished to make enough money to buy a ticket to travel back to Bramka, where Looking Ahead Orphanage was, but people weren't giving too much, and he needed money to buy food and water as well, so he had to live basically on what he was getting from people.

Chapter 9. Where Could He Be?

"Train up a child in the way he should go, and when he is old he will not depart from it" (Proverbs 22:6).

It was Friday morning, and Roger and the team of supervisors met for breakfast at the hotel's restaurant named "Comfy Restaurant," at the same place they had spent the night. They paid for only one night for four rooms, each in his/her own room, and they didn't think they would have to come back to it as they were hoping to find James this time.

On Thursday night, Martha prayed for about two hours and trusted James in God's hands. She prayed for protection over him and also protection for the children from the orphanage so that this would not happen again. Her prayer was: *"Thank You, Heavenly Father, that You are the one taking care of James. Even though he might be without any hope, please help him feel secure. Please provide for his needs and help him to have some food and water. I pray You will give us wisdom on how to look for him. Please let us find him and be able to take care of him again. Please forgive us for not being so responsible and not taking him back to the orphanage with us on Wednesday. Please bless the orphanage, and I trust all ninety-nine that are there now in your hands. Help us to be more responsible for each of these children and take care more of them. Please give us Your blessing in finding James. Thank You that You have all the power in Heaven and on earth and that, in Your providence, you will take care of James' needs and help him to be safe..."*

She prayed for about two hours and was comforted that God is in control and that, in His providence, He would provide for James.

While they were eating breakfast at Comfy Restaurant, they made a plan for that day. They were happy that they all had a driver's license, so they made a plan that two of them, Roger and Samantha, would drive for a few hours around the city and try to look for James. The other two, Martha and Joe, would walk separately on a large area and look for James. They were happy about the plan and thought that it might be more efficient this way. Roger said that if this day would be unsuccessful again that he would let authorities know in the evening and ask for their help in finding James.

As they were eating, Martha couldn't stop thinking about James and if he had anything to eat. She said to the others: "I'm so sorry for our James! I hope he has something to eat now! I know that God will provide!"

"You speak with so much certainty, Martha! How do you know?" Roger said.

"Yes, God is certainly in control. I prayed for James, and I know that He will provide for him, in His own ways and in His own timing."

"Thank you for praying for him! You see, I'm so busy with running the orphanage and with so many responsibilities that I don't really make time for going to Church, even though deep in my heart I know I should go there more!" Roger said.

Joe and Samantha were just listening in to this conversation with great interest.

"You know, people can get very busy in this life, doing things for themselves, they need to eat, to get dressed, to have a shelter, but they center their lives around all these things that will one day perish. And what will happen to them, where will they spend their eternity?" Martha added.

"Yes, I do spend a lot of time for myself and for providing for my family," Roger said.

"It is never too late to put God in the first place in your life. God can help you accomplish this if you trust your life in his hands." Martha added.

"My grandmother is a Christian as well! She loves God with all her heart and prays a lot for my family. I sometimes went with her to church, especially when I was a child, but then I didn't go so much, especially after I moved to Bramka for studying at college," Samantha confessed to them.

"God loves us so much! He gave everything for us! Why shouldn't we love Him and choose Him as well? He wants the best for us. After trusting my life to God, He helped me and modeled me more. I'm not perfect, but God sees me perfect through Jesus. He forgave my sins, and He gave me abundant joy in my heart! I read the Bible a lot, and it is very beneficial to me!" Martha said.

"Yes, I noticed a change in you! You are happier, and you no longer look so worried like before!" Joe added.

“Thank you, Joe! It’s a peace that only God put in my heart! Naturally, I tend to worry a lot, about almost anything, but knowing that God is in control makes me have more peace in my heart. I just trust myself in His hands, through prayer, and I trust my worries in His hands as well!” Martha said.

“I wish I could be like you!” Samantha said.

“Samantha, I’m happy that you said that! You need to ask for God’s help, and He will be there for you,” Martha said.

“That sounds so easy! I’m sorry I didn’t do this earlier in my life!” Samantha said.

God was using Martha in such a great way. She spoke about God with so much joy and testified His love to her classmates. And Samantha’s grandmother’s prayers were finding an answer through Martha’s encouragement.

“I would like to invite all three of you to come on Sunday to Church! I would be very happy if you were able to come! Roger, you can invite your wife as well, if she would like to!” Martha said.

“Sounds like a plan!” everyone agreed.

"OK, that will do! I will ask Elisabeth, as well if she would like to come with me!" Roger added.

"Wow, what a wonderful way God is working!" Martha was thinking about God with so much gratefulness in her heart.

After talking a little bit more and finishing with breakfast, the team split as they planned and went on to look for James.

Martha and Joe started to walk in Providence, each on his or her own way to cover a larger area. They were looking at people on streets to try and find James. They went into some stores as well and looked for him. They asked people if they saw a boy alone, and they described him.

Also, Roger and Samantha drove while carefully looking on the streets and different places around the city. They drove two separate cars so that they could cover a bigger area.

The team knew how big the city was and the fact that the boy could be just anywhere. They knew how hard this task would be for them, but they still tried to find him, because they really cared about him, just as they cared about the rest ninety-nine other children that were staying at the orphanage.

As Martha was looking for James in Providence walking on her own, she had plenty of time to think as well. In her heart, Martha was thinking about the lost sheep story from the Bible. She felt like going after James was like going after the lost sheep. She was sorry that she and Samantha, along with Joe, did not show full responsibility on the trip to the zoo on Children's Day and got back to the orphanage without James.

Martha felt how important James was, especially after not having him with them anymore. She cared for all one hundred children, but she and other three people from the orphanage left all the other ninety-nine children with the rest of the staff while they focused their full energy on finding James.

She was thinking how important every sheep was to the shepherd who had one hundred sheep. He loved and cared for each them, but when one was lost, he focused on finding that particular one. It didn't matter for him which one, he didn't show a preference for a particular sheep; he showed how much he cared for all by going after that one which was missing. It could have been any one of those one hundred sheep.

Same for the orphanage children. It could have been any other child in James' place. They would have done the same, for sure, go after him and try to find him and bring him/her back to a safer place, which was the orphanage in their case.

Chapter 10. Meanwhile at the Orphanage

"Now this is the confidence that we have in Him, that if we ask anything according to His will, He hears us" (1 John 5:14).

Since Emma alerted Martha and Roger over the phone on the night of April 2nd, the children were on alert as well, as they discovered that one of them was no longer there. Still, many of them were extremely tired after such a long day and went to bed, very soon after they heard the news.

Others didn't know how they could help to find James, but they were very concerned and showed how much they cared about him. Among them was Jason, James' best friend from the orphanage.

The children couldn't help much in the search, unfortunately. They were told that people are going to search for James in Providence and that they shouldn't worry about it. Roger didn't want to make a big deal out of this either so that news broadcasters would not come and question how things operate at the orphanage. Roger knew, deep in his heart, that many things could be improved at the orphanage, so he was trying to avoid a serious inspection on it, as that would really make him concerned.

If until now the children didn't notice James too much, his absence was now noticed, and the children talked more about him and were very worried about him. They were wondering where he could be, what he was eating, where was he sleeping, or if something bad happened to him. They had all kinds of thoughts.

Jason tried to be calm and trust James in God's hands. He was praying for him a lot. He was glad that he became a Christian, and he knew that, in God's providence, God would provide. He didn't lose hope that if God wanted James back at the orphanage, He would bring James back to the orphanage. Jason knew how mighty God really is, so he didn't lose hope. He knew that God could turn this not-so-good situation into something very good. God can do anything; that is one thing for which Jason was sure!

Jason initiated a prayer group as well, along with Kathy, Bob, and Matt, the ones that gave their lives to Jesus as well. They met in the morning after breakfast and in the evening after dinner. Also, they prayed for him in their individual times as well.

All of them loved God a lot, and since giving their hearts to Jesus, a journey with God had started for them. They were growing spiritually day by day, and they were excited and encouraged about how strong God is. In a sense, they were like the early Church, in the book of Acts, when the Church was growing more and more spiritually and meeting daily together. While the Church where they attended didn't meet daily, these Christians at the orphanage became more and more excited about God's provision and care, especially through reading more about Him from the Bible and through their own daily personal experiences. They all had their own Bibles, which they got from the church they attended with the group of missionaries.

The group of missionaries found out as well about what happened from the orphanage staff. They were amazed at first, because of the unexpected news, but then they knew what they should do. They also prayed for James, both individually and in their group. Also, because the staff was shortened because of Roger's, Samantha's, Martha's, and Joe's unexpected search throughout the city of Providence, the missionaries volunteered to help out at the orphanage until things were better and James was home. It was a very nice gesture from their side, and they called Roger and talked to him about this. Roger was extremely glad of their support.

Chapter 11. A Rise of Hope

"All we like sheep have gone astray; We have turned, every one, to his own way; And the Lord has laid on Him the iniquity of us all" (Isaiah 53:6).

James felt lost in the big city of Providence. It was the third day for him of being there on his own since Wednesday evening, and it was already Friday evening, and he was still alone.

He had a rough day on Friday. He kept Buddy in his arms, and he went along. He kept begging from people either on the streets or inside stores or restaurants. He was rejected many times, and he felt many times disappointed, but he had the strength to move on, even though he didn't know how he was able to move on after all that was happening to him. He was also surprised at how much energy he had with tiny amounts of food.

He went into restaurants to ask for people for some food and was thrown out regularly, but he was starving, so he kept trying.

"Go out from here! Look for food in a different place! Don't you ever come back here!" different people said to him, especially restaurant owners or other staff members.

"Please, give me some food! A piece of bread or anything else!" James said to them.

"Go from here! Don't ask us, ask someone else!" was a response he many times got.

He went on, and on, having so many rejections on the way and feeling so helpless, and so hungry.

When he got to Purple Diamond Restaurant, which was a very exclusive restaurant, he found very few people inside the restaurant. The staff was very busy, so he wasn't noticed from the beginning. He got to a table where a married couple was eating peacefully. Her name was Sarah, and his name was Timothy. They were having a very special meal, and seemed to enjoy the time they were spending together, when James came to them, and said, "Please have mercy on me! I am so hungry, and I have no food! Could I have something from you? Anything would be good for me!"

The next moment, two staff members pulled him aside and said to him: "Go away from here, little boy!" one employee said.

"Go and find another place to beg, not here!" the other employee said.

The woman, Sarah, reacted to their outrage, saying, "How dare you treat him in this manner?"

The two waiters were completely shocked by the lady's reaction, and they apologized to her and to the boy as well. James didn't expect anything good to happen anyway, and he was already used to such treatments from many other places, but this time he was amazed at how the lady was on his side and was defending him.

When things settled down, and staff members felt sorry for what they did, the woman then invited James to sit down at their table and asked him what he would like to eat.

James said: "Even a piece of bread would be so good for me right now! I'm just so very hungry! Thank you so much for your kindness!"

Sarah saw how humble he was in his request, and she chose a very good meal for him: two fried chicken legs with mashed potatoes and a mixed salad. James was constantly amazed by how well he was being treated by this lady and her husband. Both Timothy and Sarah were very nice to him. They didn't look at his dirty clothes or at how poor he was; instead, they looked at him through the eyes of Christ, in the sense that God loves the world so much that He cares for every sinner and He wants sinners to be saved.

Timothy and Sarah were a very nice Christian married couple. They had been married for twenty years, and it was their anniversary celebration that they were having that evening.

"OK, tell us more about you. What's your name and where are you from? Tell us more about your family as well. I'm sure they are worried about you," Sarah said to James.

"My name is James. I'm from the city of Bramka, and I grew up in Looking Ahead Orphanage," James said to them.

And then he went on, explaining more about how he got to be alone in Providence, and how much he missed the orphanage, because he had food there, a rather comfortable bed, lots of children. He also mentioned that his heart's desire was to be adopted by a real family and how much that would mean to him.

As he was talking and explaining things from his life, and how he felt as an orphan boy, lost in an unknown city, Sarah felt very sorry for him.
She already wanted to adopt him, deep in her heart, but she knew that she would first need to discuss with Timothy, her husband, as well. They already had ten children at home, and they both liked children a lot. They enjoyed rearing them up and giving them a good Christian education.

For them, the spiritual investment in their children was so important, and they liked to keep God in the first place in their lives. They were themselves a real example for their children and a true model to follow.

Sarah knew that James didn't have a place to sleep, so she talked with her husband quietly, while James was eating, and they both decided that it was a good idea to invite him to spend that night at their home, and then they would see what they would do next.

James couldn't express how grateful he was to be able to go to sleep in a different place other than outside in the city on a hard bench.

"Thank you so much! That is very kind from your side!" James said to them.

"You're very welcome!" both of them said to him.

Timothy paid for the meal, and then all three went to Timothy and Sarah's home by car together. They arrived in about ten minutes...

Chapter 12. Insight into a Big, Happy Family

"Give us this day our daily bread" (Matthew 6:11).

Even though James didn't see the whole picture from the beginning, God was in control. God was taking care of him, in His providence.

He had to face some trials, but even those trials weren't so big so that He couldn't help James. God didn't allow anything bad to happen to James, and even though people were rejecting him many times and throwing him out, even though his drawings and tools were stolen one time, even though he had to suffer from hunger a few times, James was still safe and healthy.

He just arrived on Friday night at Sarah's and Timothy's home. They had ten children. While they were gone to the Purple Diamond Restaurant, they had a babysitter to take care of children, as ages ranged between three and sixteen. They had a set of twins as well, who were nine years old, two boys: Josh and Jimmy.

They had well-behaved children, and seven of them already accepted Christ as their Lord and Savior. Only the three little children, hadn't yet: Jessica, the three years old one, Betty, the five years old one, and Kaleb, the eight years old one.

Timothy and Sarah had four girls and six boys. They loved their children a lot.

Sarah mainly stayed at home, taking care of their children and their home full-time. She had a Social Worker degree and had worked for two years at a state orphanage in Providence. After getting married to Timothy and having children, that was her primary responsibility. Priorities changed in her life, and family was more important to her. She still visited the children at the orphanage in Providence when she could.

They raised their children with the mindset of looking after the poor, being generous and giving. They focused a lot on character development with their children, knowing how important this aspect is in life, emphasizing integrity as an essential trait.

Timothy was a business man. He had completed studies in Management and opened a small business after the first five years of marriage. He had a lot of managerial experience from before, as he worked in several other companies in Financial Management and other similar roles. He had a strong knowledge of what it took to open a business and opened the business with two other former classmates from his Bachelor's Management class.

They had opened a Christian bookstore, and it grew over the years into a large store chain, with similar replications in five other cities in the country of Graceland. Many Christian authors got their books in the bookstore, and they even had a book publisher for authors who chose to publish through them. Their business was run with integrity, and they trusted the business in God's hands, who blessed them and allowed the business to grow a lot.

Unfortunately, Timothy had to travel away from home sometimes, for at least a few days each month. They had a lot of work all over the country, and the expansion of the business meant less time with his family. Still, when he was at home, he was entirely disconnected from business matters and wanted to give his full attention to his family. They had, in this way, precious moments as a family, and very many happy memories.

Due to the successful business, God helped them financially as well, so that even though the number of family members increased over the years, they had plenty of resources and didn't have days without bread on the table, only by God's grace.

Timothy was a very humble man, even though he was very successful. He knew that God deserved all the glory for all of his success; because of his attitude, he had many opportunities to witness about God to people on many different occasions. When he was asked by individual people, television stations, radio stations, and various organizations about how he managed to be so successful, he affirmed again and again that God is good and that He provides.

Some people, understanding more how great God is, they turned to follow Him as well, because through his testimonies he wasn't attributing all the merits to himself but to the One who is worthy of praise.

James noticed as well that Timothy praised God in his talking. James felt very welcome in Timothy and Sarah's family. When James arrived, the children treated him well and made him feel comfortable. He felt something that he didn't feel before, a peace and comfort by being in a family environment.

In his heart, James wished so much that he would have had such a nice family like this one. But he realized that he had to be realistic in his heart and not forget that he was only invited to spend one night there, that it wasn't his life. Still, he was very thankful for what he had and for their hospitality.

James was allowed to take a bath and was given clean clothes from one of the boys his age. He slept in the same room with the twins, Josh and Jimmy; the twins shared the same bed that night and allowed James to sleep on the other one. He really felt like part of the family now, but in his mind, he just wasn't sure what the next day would hold...

Chapter 13. Feeling Overly Blessed

"When my father and my mother forsake me, Then the Lord will take care of me" (Psalm 27:10).

After saying good night to all eleven children, including James, Timothy and Sarah went to their room. They started to talk about James: "I'm so sorry for James!" Sarah said to Timothy.

"Yes, I know! It's not easy to live on the streets, even if only for a few days!" Timothy replied.

"Timothy, I have been thinking a lot about James, especially since we got home and saw how well he fits into our family! I feel led by God to discuss with you about adopting him! I prayed in my mind as God was leading me towards this step, and I would like to know what do you think about it!" Sarah said.

"Sarah, I think we are on the same page on this! I feel the same. I know nothing is a coincidence, and I also feel led by God towards adopting James! I really like him; he is very nice, and I was amazed today for how grateful he was for everything he got, even though he is not a Christian yet!"

"I'm so happy, Timothy! I'm so glad God spoke to your heart as well! You are the best husband in the whole world! You are just so perfect for me!"

"I love you so much, Sarah! And I'm so blessed to have you in my life! Happy twenty years of marriage! And what a wonderful gift God blessed us with on this anniversary, to send James our way! And, I am already so thankful to Him for all of our ten children! God is so wonderful!" Timothy said to his wife.

Both of them were very happy, thinking that they can be a blessing for James and provide a family to him, one that he so much needs.

They prayed before going to bed, as they usually did every night, and trusted their family, including all their children, in God's hands. They prayed specifically for James, as well, that He would bless them as they planned to take on this big step of adoption. They prayed that everything would work out well and that they would get along well with James and be a good family for him.

They would let James know in the morning, along with everyone else, at breakfast.

That night, James had a very good sleep, even though before going to bed he didn't know what the next day would bring. He thought about how hard it would be to go back on the streets and start begging all over again.

James also thought about how nice Timothy and Sarah were to him. He felt like he was treated extremely nice and he couldn't be anything else but very grateful.

In the morning, which was Saturday, the family gathered to have breakfast together. James was also invited, and he was very happy about it, even though he was thinking that this might be the last meal with this very nice family before going back to the streets of Providence.

Timothy said the blessing for the food: *"Dear Heavenly Father, Thank you so much for the way that you provide for our daily needs, and thank you that we have bread on the table for today, as well as so many more food options. We are very thankful, God! Please bless this day, bless Sarah and me, and all of our children. Please bless James as well! Thank You for Your providence! You deserve all the glory!*

In Jesus' name we pray, Amen."

"Enjoy the meal!" Timothy said to everyone.

"Thank you! Enjoy the meal!" many replies came back.

They had cereal with milk. They also had bread with butter, cheese, ham, tomatoes, and cucumbers. They had fruits and yogurts available as well. They usually could choose what they would eat, depending on each person's preference. They had a choice of water, milk, juice, and tea as well.

To his surprise, James didn't know that a meal could contain so many options. He was overwhelmed. He didn't have too much food while being on the streets and when he was at the orphanage, they didn't have an extensive variety of options. For breakfast, they had either an omelet with bread or a sandwich, with a choice of tea or water to drink. They rarely had cereal with milk for breakfast, even though that was one of his main preferences.

While James was eating with much enthusiasm, Timothy spoke out with joy to everyone:

"Dear James, and dear children! We would like to make a very special announcement today! Your Mom and I have decided, as led by God, to start the process to adopt James into our family!"

"Hurray!" the children exclaimed happily...

James was shocked. He looked at Timothy, and it was like a dream for him. He wasn't sure if it is real or just a dream, so he decided to pinch himself. He felt the pinch, so he knew right away how real everything was. He still couldn't believe it. Timothy and Sarah looked at James, as he didn't say anything for about thirty seconds after the announcement was made. He was just looking at them, trying to figure out how real everything was.

Timothy decided to again say something: "Yes, James! We would like to be your family, by God's grace! He has provided for you in His Sovereignty and led your steps so that we would meet you in the Purple Diamond Restaurant! I know it is a little bit early for you to decide if this is what you would like as well, so you can take your time to think about it if you want!" Timothy said.

"Oh, wow! This is my biggest dream, and I'm just amazed that it is coming true! Thank you so much!

You are so nice to me! Does this mean that I will live here with you all?" James said.
"Yes, this is what it means, although we must respect the formalities of officially adopting you as well, with all the necessary related paperwork. But from now on, please call me Dad! We will treat you as one of our children!" Timothy replied.

"James, it is an honor for us that God has led you to us. We want to take care of you, just like we take care of everyone else within our family. And, please call me Mom!"

"Thank you... Mom... and Dad!" he said with a little bit of hesitation, but much joy as he never said these words to anyone else before.

The children were happy to have a new brother. The older ones were used to welcoming new children into their family, as almost every year there was a newborn child within the family. They were strong and united as siblings and ready to welcome James into their family as their brother.

James couldn't express the joy in his heart and how overwhelmed he was with all this wonderful news. He liked this family a lot, and he was very happy that he could be a part of it. He was so happy that he didn't need to go back on the streets, and he decided to show gratefulness and to be an obedient child in this new family.

Chapter 14. The Lost is Found

"And when he comes home he calls together his friends and neighbors, saying to them, 'Rejoice with me, for I have found my sheep which was lost!'"
(Luke 15:6)

After long searches that Roger's team did to find James, because of no results yet, Roger decided to call the police and ask for their help. James was already missing for more than forty-eight hours now, so they should be open to help.

Roger and the team stopped the searches at eight on Friday evening. He said to the team: "I'm afraid I'll have to let the authorities know that we are missing James! He could be anywhere by now, and he might even be in danger! We need some more help!"

"It is such a hard decision, but I think it is the best!" Samantha agreed.

Both Martha and Joe agreed as well.

They were all willing to go and search for him in the big city of Providence, but they had searched for two days in a row already and hadn't found James yet. They hadn't lost their hopes, they just needed to have some more help. With authorities in charge as well, they might find James a lot easier and a lot quicker.

After Roger called the Providence Police Department and gave to them all the details they asked for, they let him know that they would start working on this case on Saturday morning.

The Providence Police Department was very well trained and had plenty of police officers who had answered the calling of working in the police department in order to serve, protect, and help the citizens. Lieutenant Gray, the one who responded to the call, had many successful cases already in his history of over thirty years in this field. He and his team were specialized in finding missing people as well.

Lieutenant Gray assured Roger that he would handle this case with his team with a big responsibility and that he hopes that the boy is safe and that he will soon return to the orphanage.

Little did Roger know that God had other plans for James... He would only find out in the morning how God had provided for James.

The team had dinner together and discussed how the day went on. They found it to be a very hard job to keep looking for a missing person, but it was worth it, they did this for James.

Martha kept praying a lot for James and had him mainly in her prayers. She knew that God would provide.

They had requested help from the police department, so they made plans and were to discuss details during breakfast time, on Saturday morning.

While they were having breakfast, Roger gets a phone call. Thinking that it might be Lieutenant Gray or someone else from the police department, he was quick to respond.

"Hello! Good morning!" Roger said, very politely.
"Hi, is this Mr. Roger Parkinson, from Looking Ahead Orphanage in Bramka?"

When Roger heard that he was called about something related to the orphanage, he wasn't sure how to react. He knew that his cell phone is not available to the public and he asked the staff to handle any calls from outside that would come in his name so that he could focus more on finding James and not be disturbed by a multitude of calls. He was on the phone with this gentleman, so he decided to continue the conversation, even though he wanted to keep it short.

"Yes, my name is Roger! How can I help you?" he said.

After presenting who he is, Timothy said, "I'm calling you regarding James." He said this with a very soft voice that expressed a lot of calm and peace.

Roger didn't know what to think when he heard that. He thought that maybe the issue is public now and many others know about the fact that James is missing. He wasn't sure why this man called him.

"Yes, I'm listening," Roger said, trying to maintain his voice calm.

"Mr. Parkinson, I'm calling you to ask for your permission to adopt James," Timothy said.

Roger was thinking that this wasn't the right time for such a question - right now, when James is missing, someone wants to adopt him. He didn't know how to handle this, so he said:

"I'm afraid that this is not possible. We don't know where he is," Roger said.

"He is with our family now. He came to ask for food last night, while my wife and I were at a restaurant," Timothy continued and explained the whole situation, how they met James.

"Wow, that is the best news I've gotten this entire year! Thank you, Sir! I'm so glad he is safe!" Roger said when he heard that James is OK.

Roger asked where they could meet to discuss further and also meet the family that wants to adopt James. In the meantime, when Samantha, Martha, and Joe were listening to this phone conversation, they understood that James was found, and they were so happy. They didn't get the whole story yet, so they thought that maybe the police department already found him. They thought that the police department was indeed very fast.

Timothy gave Roger all the details where he lives, and he said that they could meet that day as he was off that Saturday from work and Roger could meet his wife and children as well. After agreeing on all the details, they hung up their phones.

Roger couldn't wait to let everyone know about this very good news.

"James was found!" he said very happily.

"Thank God!" Martha exclaimed.

"Wow, that is so wonderful!" Samantha said.

"That is excellent news! You have made my day! I am so happy!" Joe said with a lot of joy in his heart.

After giving more details to them, Roger called the police department as well, to let them know that James had been found.

Martha asked to pray and praise God for what He did. Out of respect and gratitude, they all bowed down their heads, as she prayed:

"Thank you, Heavenly Father. You have shown a lot of mercy to us by helping us today to find James, through this man, Timothy, and his family. Please bless them, we pray! Thank you that, in your providence, you have been in control of James' life. Please continue to bless him! You deserve all the glory for everything!

In Jesus' name we pray, Amen."

Roger had to go and meet with Timothy. The other three asked for permission to go with him. Timothy thought it would be a good thing if they went together.

Chapter 15. Rejoice

"Rejoice in the Lord always. Again I will say, rejoice!" (Philippians 4:4)

The true happiness and rejoicing for the lost one who was found was from the moment they met at Timothy's home. After greeting Timothy, his wife, and their children, Roger looked at James and noticed how well he was, even after a few days in loneliness. God had been so good to him!

"Hi James, I'm so glad you are doing good! We have been looking for you a lot, these days," Roger said softly, with abundant joy in his heart to see him again safe, while giving him a big hug.

"Hello, Mr. Parkinson! Please forgive me that I ran away like that! I'm very sorry! I made a big mistake, from which I have learned a lot!" James said.

Roger was thinking about James' words. He didn't realize until then that actually James planned his escape and it wasn't just the negligence of the staff as he thought before.

"Hi James, I'm so happy to see you! God has provided, and you are OK! Praise God!" Martha said while greeting James and hugging him warmly.

Samantha and Joe did the same, and James felt loved and appreciated. He missed them a lot as well! He indeed had learned his lesson.

"Timothy, I understood from you over the phone that you would like to adopt James! I'm afraid that James will have to come back to the orphanage and afterward we can start the adoption process," Roger said.

"OK, I understand that there is a process! Let us know all the details that we need to know from our side so that this process goes smoothly!" Timothy said to him.

"We also appreciate all that you did for James and the fact that you want to take him into your family! I can see that you have a wonderful family!" Roger said while looking at Timothy's ten children.

Timothy and his wife invited them to stay over for lunch, and they discussed a little bit more with the orphanage staff and knew each other more.

Timothy blessed the food, and then they started to eat.

"You are a great cook!" Samantha said to Sarah, as she was enjoying the meal a lot.

"Thank you! I appreciate it!" Sarah said to her.

"Yes, the food is excellent!" Joe said to Sarah.

Sarah cooked spaghetti with chicken breast and tomato sauce with mushrooms, as she knew how much her children like that meal, so she decided to have it cooked for the guests as well that day.

After lunch, Roger took James back to the orphanage along with Joe, while Samantha and Martha drove separately in the second car they had with them.

Saying goodbye to such a wonderful family was hard to James, but he didn't forget their desire to adopt him, so, deep in his heart, he knew that he would return to them, which made him happy and very encouraged. He liked the orphanage much better than the life on the streets, as he had now what to compare the orphanage life with, but having the opportunity to belong to such a nice family meant so much to him.

Timothy, Sarah, and all ten children said goodbye to James as he went back to the orphanage until the adoption procedure was started. They said that he would be missed during this time and that they were looking forward to his return soon.

James still held his stuffed bear tightly in his arms. He had tears in his eyes as he had to say bye to such wonderful people. He couldn't wait until he is back again and live with them. He felt very blessed to have such a great family, and he was encouraged in his heart by God.

On the way back, Roger called the orphanage staff in Bramka and asked them to prepare a very good meal with the special occasion of having James back safe. They wanted to rejoice together with all one hundred children and be thankful for having them all safe.

The staff was thrilled when they heard the great news of James being found and that he was coming back safely. Roger didn't mention that James was on the way of being adopted, which was also excellent news.

Roger was happy anytime someone adopted children from the orphanage. He knew that this orphanage was not the best place to live in, as any child needs someone that they can call Mom and Dad.

There were though some criteria that potential parents had to meet, among which they had to maintain a peaceful environment for good growth and development of the children. If the family didn't get along very well, they were not eligible to get another member into their family, as a rule of the orphanage. This is one of the big reasons why only a few of the children had been adopted, even though more families would have been willing to do so without considering how important the family environment is for children.

Roger always thought that children are very valuable, so when children were placed with families, he wanted to make sure that they found good families for them.

When, after a very long drive, Roger got back with James and the team to the orphanage, they had a very nice surprise waiting for them... balloons everywhere, happy children that went to greet and hug James, children's music, and pizza to celebrate the event, which was one of the children's favorite meals.

James felt very happy and loved by everyone. The children and staff were so happy to see him back. Some had been worried about him during the time he was missing; others, like Jason, tried not to worry, but instead prayed for James and knew that God would provide.

James was so glad to see Jason again. They really were best friends. Jason said to James that he was praying for him a lot. James thanked him for that.

God had been working a lot in James' heart during this time. He helped him learn valuable lessons, and, in his time of loneliness, which wasn't so long, he was more appreciative and full of gratitude for things he was taking for granted. It had only taken three days for James to learn things that built his character. God was shaping him into the man He desired him to become.

It was a moment full of rejoicing when James met again with orphanage staff and all the other ninety-nine children. What a special time they had. It was a very nice celebration, and James was so welcomed.

In the middle of it, Roger made the very special announcement to all of them:

"We are so happy to have James back here, even if this is just for a very short time, it seems..."

Everyone was paying a lot of attention. They didn't understand why James was going to spend just a little time there; they thought maybe he was going to be punished and sent out from Looking Ahead Orphanage to a different orphanage or had their own thoughts about what could Roger mean by that.

But Roger continued, and he said:

"I'm pleased to announce that James will be adopted! He will be part of a very good family from Providence. So, enjoy your time together while he is still here with you!"

"Oh, wow! That's excellent news for him! I wish I would be adopted as well," many children said.

"I hope that he will still at least come to visit us once in a while! He will be greatly missed, but we are happy for him, truly happy!"

And Roger continued, by saying: "You know, dear children, you are all very important to us! We would have done the same thing for any of you if you had been the one missing. We care for you a lot, even if sometimes you might feel that we have strict rules for you here; that is still for your own good, trust me! We hope that you will all become great men and women one day, that will make this world better! You are all important, don't forget this!"

All the children felt very appreciated. It was such a nice time, and this would undoubtedly remain in their memories! Roger was very nice to them; he was almost like a father to them. He truly cared for them. He had been the director of this orphanage for over ten years already, and he knew many of them since they got there.

He was busy with a lot of paperwork and things that had to do with running the orphanage, so he didn't have so much time to spend with them each personally. He tried to have some activities that involved everyone at least once per month, like an organized soccer game or a movie evening when he brought his own projector from home and they watched a family movie together.

James had a change of perspective now. It wasn't that all things were so bad at the orphanage, but through his selfish lens, he had not been able to see how blessed he was to have all that he needed.

And now, even more than that, God had helped him to find a family that will adopt him... What a blessing for him, what a loving God that cares about him, just as He cares for all the other ninety-nine children from the orphanage!

God had worked uniquely in each person's lives, and His desire was that each of these children would come to know Him personally.

This is why he allowed for circumstances for them to hear about Him, so He sent Esther Joshua and Jonathan to witness about His love. He used their faithfulness towards Him to share the Gospel to the lost people. And yes, a few had already come to know Him.

The missionaries also rejoiced along with the staff and children. They were there to embrace James in this time of happiness, and surely they had supported him during the time of separation when James had been alone in Providence. What a support group James had, even though he didn't know about it! What a blessing from God!

Chapter 16. God at Work

"How then shall they call on Him in whom they have not believed? And how shall they believe in Him of whom they have not heard? And how shall they hear without a preacher?" (Romans 10:14)

On Sunday morning, when Martha went to Church, she had a delightful surprise. She saw Joe, Samantha, Roger, and his wife there. They all had responded positively to her invitation; God reminded them of it and searched their hearts so that they would be open about it and be able to go on Sunday.

Martha was so happy! Esther, Joshua, and Jonathan were there as well. They were doing the same thing, taking with them Jason, Kathy, Bob, and Matt, but besides them, they took James as well this Sunday, as he had seemed very willing and open to come. With Roger's approval, they took him as well.

It was such a blessed Sunday. The worship songs were lifting God's name on high, giving Him the praise that He deserves. At the prayer time, Martha prayed as well. She thanked God for the way that

He worked in James' life and for all His protection towards him.

When James heard her prayer, he was very encouraged.

The sermon was very touching as well. It was from Ephesians 2, verses 1 through 10, which says:

"And you He made alive, who were dead in trespasses and sins, in which you once walked according to the course of this world, according to the prince of the power of the air, the spirit who now works in the sons of disobedience, among whom also we all once conducted ourselves in the lusts of our flesh, fulfilling the desires of the flesh and of the mind, and were by nature children of wrath, just as the others.

But God, who is rich in mercy, because of His great love with which He loved us, even when we were dead in trespasses, made us alive together with Christ (by grace you have been saved), and raised us up together, and made us sit together in the heavenly places in Christ Jesus, that in the ages to come He might show the exceeding riches of His grace in His kindness toward us in Christ Jesus.

For by grace you have been saved through faith, and that not of yourselves; it is the gift of God, not of works, lest anyone should boast.

For we are His workmanship, created in Christ Jesus for good works, which God prepared beforehand that we should walk in them."

The pastor talked a lot about God's abundant grace towards us, through Jesus Christ, and the fact that it is not through our own merits the fact that we can be God's children; only by His grace. The pastor explained that grace means to receive an undeserved gift. We all deserved death because of our sins, but through Him we have life, as Jesus washes all of our sins through His blood, when we put our faith in Him, dedicate our lives to Him and invite Him to live within us.

Roger was paying a lot of attention and even had tears coming out from his eyes when the pastor talked about the fact that Jesus died on the cross for us, because He loves us, and through Him we have free access to the gift of eternal life.

The sermon took about forty minutes, and at the end, the pastor made an invitation to come in the front of the Church for all those who don't have

Jesus as their Lord and Savior yet but would like to make Him their Lord and Savior.

Martha was praying during this time; she brought into God's attention Roger and his wife, in addition to Samantha and Joe as well. She prayed for James as well, that God would work in his heart and bless him with salvation.

When Martha looked up to see who was in front, she saw Roger there. She was so happy for him. God had worked in his life and changed his heart for His glory. She was praying for him in her heart that he is going to follow Him with faithfulness. What a wonderful Sunday. They all liked it at Church, and Roger had decided to follow God.

God used Roger to be a better director at the orphanage and to be a better support of the missionaries that came to help the children. He became a supporter of the children going to Church, and that became part of the orphanage's policy. Children started to benefit more and more from Roger's dedication to Christ. They saw the difference, and Roger was more involved in talking to the children and spending more quality time with them.

Chapter 17. Happy Adoption Day

"Do all things without complaining and disputing, that you may become blameless and harmless, children of God without fault in the midst of a crooked and perverse generation, among whom you shine as lights in the world, holding fast the word of life, so that I may rejoice in the day of Christ that I have not run in vain or labored in vain" (Philippians 2:14-16).

Timothy and Sarah had bought another bed and put it in the same room with their twins, Josh and Jimmy, for James. They bought different things for him that he would need when he came to stay with them.

Roger started the adoption process first thing on Monday morning. He called Timothy to let him know what documents he needed to bring with him when he came to pick up James from the orphanage. Roger said that he could come on Tuesday to take him to his new home. Timothy was happy to hear that.

Timothy and Sarah were delighted to have him part of the family, especially since they both felt led by God to take on this step. They felt honored that God sent James their way, in His providence; they also were thinking how many things might have happened to him in being alone at seven years old in such a big city like Providence. Only God took care of him in such a wonderful way and made sure to keep him safe all these days that he was just wandering around by himself. Even though James didn't know it, God was with him.

It was April 8th, Tuesday morning, when Timothy drove to Bramka to Looking Ahead Orphanage. He took off for that particular day, from work.

Sarah gave Timothy some snacks and sweets that James could enjoy on the long way back home from Bramka to Providence. She had to stay home to take the older ones to school and stay with the little ones at home.

She also prepared a small surprise party for when James was officially part of the family and invited relatives and friends to come and join them to make it a happy and enjoyable adoption day.

Timothy arrived at the orphanage at 12:30 pm. He went to discuss with Roger and fill out some paperwork. A lawyer had come to the orphanage to make the adoption official, and Timothy signed the paperwork in front of the lawyer for James to be taken home to his family. The lawyer left the orphanage as soon as the paperwork was signed and after he had congratulated Timothy on the adoption of James. Timothy had certain things to do officially afterward as well, but he could already have James with him at home, not having to return him again to the orphanage. James was officially Timothy's son that day. Timothy, as James' new father, went to him and said: "Son, I'm very glad to see you! It's time for you to come home now!"

For James, everything was so new. He never had a family before; Timothy was so kind to him, and the words he was using to talk with him were so nice. He was very enthusiastic about this significant change in his life and indeed very thankful for it in his heart. He finally had what he desired so much in his heart, a family.

Timothy held James' hand and helped him with his luggage. It was time for James to say bye to all the children and the staff. Some were crying because they would miss him so much, but Timothy said that James can come and visit them sometimes.

The hardest goodbye was to his best friend, Jason. He wished him well and God's blessings upon his life: "James, I'm truly glad for you! I wish you well and may God bless you abundantly! I hope we can see each other again sometime!"

"Thank you, Jason! I will miss you!"

They both had tears in their eyes, but James knew he now had the family he had always wanted, so he went on. He wished in his heart that Jason would be a part of that family as well and be his big brother like he had always been. James truly considered Jason his "older brother" and best friend. He was there for him when he felt no one else cared so much, and he truly appreciated that, especially after coming back from Providence and understanding things better.

Timothy was happy to meet Jason, and he saw how well he and James got along together. On the way back to his new home in Providence, James was with his new father in the car. During part of the long trip back, they listened to children's Christian music and Christian stories that they had on CD.

Also, Timothy talked to him about God. It was like a man to man conversation. Timothy told James his testimony of how he met Christ. He said: *"I was raised in a non-Christian family. My parents didn't go to Church and had been busy with different things from this world.*

"My father was a businessman. He had a consultancy business, meaning that he advised people who owned different businesses in how to lead them better and be more efficient. He was very busy and traveled a lot, so he wasn't too much time at home... Unfortunately, while I was growing up, I didn't have the chance to spend too much quality time with him.

"My mom was mainly at home, taking care of us. I have three younger brothers, and I'm the oldest of four. One day, one of my high-school classmates invited me to a youth event at the Church he was attending. I wasn't too interested at first, but then I said in my heart that I would go to see what this event is about, just out of curiosity.

"I went, and it really was an enjoyable experience. The youth that I met at Church seemed to be very different than the youth I was having as friends, I noticed the difference right away, even when I looked at them, they looked so happy, smiling and

with a lot of peace in their hearts that was visible outside. I was amazed!

"They welcomed me very well and talked to me kindly. I made some new friends on the spot there. It was so easy to talk to them, I felt. The youth event started with some snacks and soft drinks. It was a good time for socializing, something that they called fellowship. They didn't judge me that I wasn't a Christian like them; instead, they welcomed me very well.

"During the actual youth service, God searched my heart through every single thing that was happening: prayer time, worship songs, and through the sermon, where He spoke to my heart directly. I understood that I am a sinner and that I needed Christ in my life, so I decided to follow Him right then.

"My life changed step by step after this big decision to follow Christ. I went to Church more often, and I even got a Bible as a gift from the friend who invited me to Church. Through reading it, I learned more about God, and day by day I grew more spiritually. I had a real thirst for going to Church, reading the Bible, and praying to God. I was so in love with God,

my Savior. I didn't recognize myself either. It was God who transformed me through His power.

"At my baptism, when I declared my faith publicly, I invited my entire family to come. My father couldn't come, as he was out of the city, busy with his own consultancy business. My mom and my three brothers came, and it was their first time to be there. It was a time that God used to search their hearts as well. They all came to Christ on that particular day. I had been praying for them before, and I was so happy to see how wonderfully God worked.

"Afterwards, the family environment changed as well. We were a Christian family, almost entirely, except my father. We prayed a lot for him together. We prayed even for his business so that he would spend more quality time with us. God was working in my family.

"After about three years my father's business went bankrupt, and he got a job that allowed him to spend more time with us. He didn't have to travel in other cities anymore. It was sad that his business failed, but we were so happy about this big change because he could also come with us to Church, and by God's grace he was open to coming to Church with us.

"Two years later, he decided to follow Christ as well. It was God's victory in my family that we all became Christians.

"Later on in life, I went to a Christian college, where I met Sarah, my wife. She was studying in Social Work, while I was studying Management.

"God put us together, by His grace, and helped us become a family together through marriage. It was such a blessing for our lives. God gave us ten children, by His grace, and now He has given you to us as well, as our son. We are so happy about this, James!"

Timothy was so kind to James. He talked to him with a lot of patience and love. He talked about how wonderful God is, and how big His love is for us. He explained to him what Jesus did for us, how He died and gave Himself for our sins. He talked about salvation and abundant grace.

When James heard all these wonderful things coming from Timothy, his testimony and how wonderfully he was talking about God, he said: "What do I have to do to follow God as well?"

Timothy was so happy when he heard this from James! He found a spot to stop the car and prayed with him. James was ready to dedicate his life to Christ. Timothy helped him pray, and James repeated the words after him:

"Dear God, I understand how big Your love for me is, and I want to respond to Your love by giving my heart to You. Jesus, I ask You to be my Lord and my Savior, and I thank You for taking my life under Your control. I want to be faithful to You my entire life. Please help me to do so, by Your grace. Thank You for Your protection and for guiding my steps to You. In Jesus' name I pray, Amen."

Timothy was so happy. He couldn't wait to get to Providence to tell his wife the great news, so he called her right away and told her what happened. She was so happy as well. Her reaction, after they hung up the phones, was to bow down on her knees and give thanks to God for the wonderful way He worked in James' life.

On the rest of the way home, Timothy and his new son, James, were listening to Christian music and singing along to the ones they knew.

When they got home, they had a big surprise awaiting:

"Surprise, Surprise!" people spoke out loud.

"Happy Adoption Day!" others joined in.

James didn't expect this, but yes, that was part of being in a family.

"Wow, thank you!" James said.

He was so surprised. Many people were there: relatives from both sides of the families and some close friends as well.

They enjoyed their time together. They had food and sweets and a big welcoming cake for James, on which was written: "Happy Adoption Day!"

James was thrilled; it was indeed a very happy adoption day. He celebrated it with his new parents, new siblings, many relatives and friends of the family. He felt loved.

As an adoption gift, he got a parrot that would learn to talk, and his parents said that he could choose a name for it. James said, "I want to call him Birdie!"

He still had his stuffed bear, Buddy, with him, which was a toy, but now he had Birdie as well to play with, and that pleased him very much.

The children liked Birdie a lot, and they played around his cage. Birdie was around one year old, and he had to learn how to talk, so that was James' role. Others in the family could also teach him to talk, as he let anyone who wanted to play with him.

They gave Birdie sunflower seeds, which he enjoyed a lot. Birdie was, indeed, very friendly, and James got attached to him very fast. He liked animals and birds a lot. In fact, when his parents realized how much he loved animals, they got the annual family pass to the Providence City Zoo. Because of how many children they had, they had to pay extra for a few extra children. They went at least once a month to the zoo with all their children.

After the adoption party had ended, Timothy and Sarah showed James his room, the same as Josh and Jimmy had.

The children got used to James fast, and they liked him. Since he accepted to follow Christ, he was being transformed through His power. He was very nice and also full of appreciation for what he had, this time, knowing that all things that he had were from God. He learned more about God, and even though he was only seven years, he decided to follow Him with faithfulness.

Chapter 18. God's Providence

"The Lord your God in your midst, The Mighty One, will save; He will rejoice over you with gladness, He will quiet you with His love, He will rejoice over you with singing" (Zephaniah 3:17).

In God's providence, James had found a family that welcomed him and loved him. After about one year since Timothy and Sarah adopted James, they decided to adopt his friend Jason as well, whom James had visited once in a while. They liked Jason, especially his character, and followed the same procedure that they had followed for James and then brought him home.

Timothy and Sarah had a big and wonderful family, with twelve children, and in God's providence, He was taking care of all. The atmosphere in the home was peaceful, even though so many were part of the same big and sweet family.

They went to church together as a family, and also Timothy kept his role very well as a spiritual leader of his family. He gathered the family for an hour of fellowship with God every evening at 8:30 pm.

That was their special time together as a family, which they all enjoyed.

In God's providence, Roger, the orphanage's director, gave his heart to Christ and let God be in control as the leader of his life. He didn't want to be in charge of his own life anymore, and he understood that he needs God in his life.

Roger's life also changed within his own family. He had a wife, a son who was fifteen years old, and a daughter who was twelve years old. He understood how much he missed out on important activities within his children's lives, just because family wasn't a priority for him. He changed his lifestyle and put family nearer the top of the list, after God. Work was now in third place, so if there was an event within his own family, he tried to make sure not to miss those.

He also brought his children more often to the orphanage, and they made friends from there. They really liked these children and helped them a lot, even with their homework, and became a great support in the development of the children from the orphanage.

Roger also spent more quality time with his wife. Through his testimony and his abundant love for her, she came to know Christ as well. She dedicated her life to Christ a few weeks after Roger did. They both got baptized on the same day as a public declaration of their faith in Jesus.

Roger and his wife made a commitment to serve the Lord by giving a proper Christian education to their children and lead them as well to Him. They became better parents as they put God first in their lives.

Many changes followed in Roger's life after he sincerely gave his heart to Jesus. He let Him be in total control, and He was.

Regarding Samantha and Joe, they were hesitant that particular Sunday. God spoke to their hearts as well, but they didn't have the courage to express what they experienced by walking to the front of the Church. They remained seated, but they continued to go to Church, and God was working in their lives as well.

They understood how great God is and how much they needed Him in their lives. God loved them so much, and they could feel His abundant love.

In God's providence, Samantha and Joe dedicated their lives to Christ as well, after a few months of going to Church regularly.

They also started to know each other more, and one day, Joe asked Samantha:

"Samantha, I have seen that you have a big love for God! I see the change God's been doing in your life. All this time we have been spending more time talking to each other, and I know you more now, and I like you as a person, I really do... Would you like to be my girlfriend?" he asked her.
"Yes, I would like to!" Samantha answered to him, as she confirmed that she also liked him.

They were both singles; Joe was twenty-five years old and Samantha was twenty-two years old. After dating Samantha for seven months, Joe asked her to be his wife, which she gladly accepted. They got married within one year from the engagement, and all the children from the orphanage were invited to their wedding, including James and Jason as well. It was a happy celebration!

In the same year, two other weddings happened, at a distance of just one week each: Joshua, the missionary, married Martha; also, Esther and Jonathan, the other missionaries that served the Lord at the orphanage, got married as well.

Note from the Author

Dear Reader,

God deserves all the glory!

Are we ready to serve Him with all our heart? Are we grateful for what He has done for us through Jesus? Are we thankful for all His blessings that He pours out for us daily?

I would like to encourage you to think about what you have and thank God for what He is doing in your life.

If you are following God with all your heart, I encourage you... this is the best decision you have ever made! Keep on following Him, and may God bless you with faithfulness in following Him! May you be a great testimony to other people, as well, so that God's love will shine through you and so that others will come to know Him as well!

If you haven't decided to follow God yet, just think about it... what is it that is keeping you from doing so? I would like to encourage you to read the Bible, God's message of love for us, and there you will find hope, encouragement, and a better knowledge of

God. Rely on Him, not on yourself. Let Him work in your life daily, and may God bless you to choose Him in your life. It is not too early, nor is it too late yet, to take this step. Do not fear, God will provide!

May God bless those who have read this book. My heart's desire is that you have found hope and encouragement through the pages of this book!

God is great and is worthy of praise! May He be glorified for His providence over our lives!

Magda Woods
Author of the novel Providence: God's Care for the Lost Sheep

About the Author

Magda Woods was born in Târgu Mureş, Romania. She graduated in 2008 from Unirea High School in Târgu Mureş with a specialization in Mathematics, Computer Science, and English. She also graduated in 2011 with a Bachelor's in Management from Griffiths School of Management at Emanuel University in Oradea, Romania, and in 2013 with a Master's in Entrepreneurial Management at the same university. Providence is her first book, and she has several other books that she's working on. Magda was married to Jeremy G. Woods in August 2016 and is pregnant with their first child, due January 2018. Magda and Jeremy live in Târgu Mureş, Romania, where they own the company FaithVenture Media.

www.ingramcontent.com/pod-product-compliance
Lightning Source LLC
Chambersburg PA
CBHW072229190626
46809CB00017B/1535

* 9 7 8 6 0 6 9 4 4 4 7 1 9 *